Pell Mell

OTHER POETRY BY ROBIN BLASER

The Moth Poem, San Francisco, Open Space, 1964.
Les Chimères, San Francisco, Open Space, 1964.
Cups, San Francisco, Four Seasons, 1968.
Image-Nations 1-12, London, Ferry Press, 1974.
Image Nations 12-14, etc., Vancouver, Cobblestone, 1975.
Syntax, Vancouver, Talonbooks, 1983.
The Faerie Queen & The Park, Vancouver, Fissure Books, 1988.

PELL
MELL

ROBIN BLASER

The Coach House Press

Toronto

I want especially to thank Sharon Thesen
for her editorial insight and her care
in the preparation of the manuscript. R.B.

Published with the assistance of
the Canada Council and the
Ontario Arts Council.

Canadian Cataloguing in Publication Data

Blaser, Robin
    Pell mell

Poems.
ISBN 0-88910-339-9

I. Title.

PS8553.L37P4 1988   C811'.54   C88-094918-X
PR9199.3.B53P4 1988

for David Farwell & Rob Dunham

A Note

These poems follow a principle of *randonnée* – the random and the given of the hunt, the game, the tour. Thus, *randonnée* is another title of this book, written, so to speak, in invisible ink. These poems are also a further movement in one long work that I call *The Holy Forest*, though that need not trouble the reader before the forest is full grown. Poems called *Image-Nations* come and go throughout, never to become a complete nation. And *Great Companions* of the art of poetry, a series which begins to gather here with Pindar and Robert Duncan, will continue until their voices close *The Holy Forest*. That's the plot.

Contents

Waiting for Hours

listen, kid,
there isn't anything but art
and the effort to turn it into
the same discourse as
everything else is
scientific
angelism, disguised as
who-dun-it   after all
on art, I'm a kind of
Fibber McGee and Molly
talkin' over the horseshoe
found in 1901—and should
I find three more, we
could have a game in
the backyard—close
the closet, undisturbed by
the ten-foot pole we
wouldn't touch anything
by, if offered—oh—
the hours remind me of
thirty robins' dreams,
snowflakes as big as cigarette
papers

the best thing ever said about me
critically was 'alien exotica'
but I looked out of my eyes at
the piano shawl and wondered
how the fringe could move so
ceaselessly over the fat back
and that was supposed to stop me
dead in my tracks—my job—my
heart—and anything I ever told you
that you believed—wow—magic
and disgusting fun people, also

Skylight

shadow of a bird
                cloud
                rain
                        Dante's face in the
raindrop—clear—   strangely
did not wash away—

Cold Morning Quotations

Being is what remains, not what is   ) Hartman

The last crows that are heard are named 'Why'   ) Nietzsche

Thanatography   ) Hartman

Thanatopraxis   ) Derrida

the morning   of short
        thoughts—gifts of rest and
        difference   I stop short
the december tomatoes shine on the top of the refrigerator
        cold, barely ripe or thoughtful
the most beautiful madrigals of Monteverdi
        play their human emotion in the
        next room—an achievement at the turn
        of the next room
the *shattered marble* of my unwalled
        thought enters the Rondanini Pietá
        silently—*shaking hands of the substance*
        melt away
in the Florence Pietá, he has removed
        Mary from her place and holds Christ
        himself to his bosom

knowledge-aware, knowledge-fraught, knowledge-
persuading, the provenance of every true song
                                                turns
existence toward a thirst for superficialities

lacking a future, a past has never existed

the boy said, *'Make way for Virgil'*
enchantment of water

reality of fate—sham-infinity, sham-
timelessness, sham-seclusion
sham-divinity, sham-holiness

your path is poetry, your goal is beyond
poetry

which is called poetry, the strangest
of all human occupations, the only one
dedicated to the knowledge of death

> [fragment structures—serial poems—
> all having to do with materiality of
> form—having to do with death]

this was like a language that is
no longer a bridge between people,
like an extra-human laughter,
its range of scorn playing about
the factual worldly-estate as such,
that in reaching beyond the
realm of all things human no
longer derides humanity but simply
destroys it by exposing the nature
of the world

herds of gods, of men, of animals, of plants, herds
     of stars
containing each other   ) Broch

New Year's, 1982
> my mind goes blank, not from
> hangover—that year is hard
> to hold on to because the *maestoso*
> was missing, except for the last
> chapter of *The Death of Virgil*, read
> at 7:45 p.m.—

IMAGE-NATION 18 (an apple

the mind I want, like an
    apple, childish
I've followed every great friend
    I've known—Spicer, Duncan,
    Olson, Creeley, Zukofsky—
not to own it   I would write
    it—having slept too long,
the ferns dream as they return
    to green
out of winter   the streets shine
with oil slicks and rain
                            I
wonder,
        that words wound,
splendid gifts of guilt and wit
    Night-birds, someone said,
are those men and women who try
to force their way into the reality
of others
        the 'Old Europe,'
Sharon Thesen said, 'which endureth, parsed
                            by structuralists,'
who don't know
                Pound said,
'you have to find it'—
the structure—of life—
which means—no longer
can philosophy find it, the
mental thing about it
    so we've gone from one thing
to another
    the effort is moral—how
are you?
        you can take it and
build the rock
(the origin of the word unknown)
                you'll wobble
unless you're the crust
                    of it

LOVE is FORM
        intimacy is the loveliest
        part of thought

i.e., I am so separate a man
these days,
bending the fabric of space

universe is part of ourselves

Olson said, 'The MORAL is FORM &
        nothing else and the MORAL ACT
        is the honest—"sincere" motion in
        the direction of FORM'

'Amo o'   lead with consonants

well, so it is,
                but some stall,
most keep their seats   stave off

larkspur   standing far

God bless jazz bands everywhere

and why not know   love
    is form

'the whole question & continuing
        struggle to remain civilized'

you've got to keep it up—find
your heart in the creation   you

came from   lower middle-class
except for Sophia Nichols' dream—
her Shakespeare,

in the middle of the modern,
1945, where was it?

to have met, 1952?—'The MORAL
is FORM & nothing else
and the MORAL ACT is the
honest—'sincere' motion in the
direction of FORM'

'Form, in fact, is now definable
as tensions'

'amo o'

6 November, '82—Dream of a poem
which went   **so.......................prize**
                   ....
                   ....
                   surprise   **) in**
stanzas

so the wind does prize
the last thought
of the bow
gold, silver, brass, iron
of the air;
surprise

so the beings larger than life
prize the over and under
of light-mush
where my feet wander on;

surprise the sweet waiting a prize
of the May to December game,
the is-ain't
love of canaries circling
eyes and time,

liquid and bitter,
prize of the rainbow-shadow

draw there in the light-dark, say,
'may we be those who bring
about the transfiguration
of the world-surprise'

Fousang

You made the past
a myth of nature
or history

you said the future
would be this or
that, devouring
the unpredictable

you fell into the East
destroying an alphabet
the future disappeared
for a myriad

millennial silliness
at the heart of your notation—
I address you personally
because you have become
personal to each of us

a progression that knows
the limit and argues it
into a slime   the whole
light-body, unpredictable
terrible, sexual, torn heart
of the matter is not there
matter is not there,
                              for that

we can thank Soviets
and u.s.'s alike, who alike stand
for nothing

matter is not there—turning,
the birds of paradise grow
feet and claws—the terror
becomes elegant as in your grammar
we are cast into nothing

a banal face oozes
out of the grass, gently,
because your future will,
you say, solve it, but there
is no future unless it be
unpredictable

we are left to sift among servants,
masters, despots and slaves
maybe, one day, the concrete substance,
the community of ourselves,
unpredictable language of our
notation will return

they knew it   home
it should be and the railway
sunlit   is, after all, a destiny
everyday

*   *   *

    the bow, carvéd gold, Blake
said,
    and the four zoas

turn in the heart, turn in the

air, a big wheel

turns, a little wheel turns,

a world, the light-spur of what we meant

mistaken and right by the river,

the north of my heart, winged,
splendid, the creatures live in
their amber and earth—sapphire
and crystal   I dream the
wind, the streets, the leaves
and the bank of the river, innocent
and experienced
at the edge of it, the larks singing back
to back
                    the frosted glass,
etched with clarities, thoughts,
rhythms, because the living creatures
of centuries
                    draw the bow
a carvéd sweetness out of 6,000,000
years   the steps of the creatures, not
spectrous   neither male nor
female singing a brightening
form in the harbour, arguing these days
against the muteness

I want you to tell me how old we
are—not simply a future-form,
cut from the effort—new and
unrinsed   I want you to see
the turn of events   the horror,
the childish matches, the flow
of the effort   information is not simply
genetic, social, momentary, but strife in events
in the earth—
unorganized—brilliant, beautiful—
the heart of the matter   unfolds matter

the living creatures stomp on the earth,
tell it, repeat, enter the shine
of
    how old we are

back to back the larks sing, back
to back the creatures sing, back
to back, the beginning and the
end of it—out of it, the
light-patches of a crazy-quilt
arrange, derange, a range
of the movement—lifted, so that,
at one moment end and beginning meet
full of laughter

you will think backwards of the beast
of ourselves, not forwards—not out of reaction,
but out of primordial surmise
                              thought as of a violet,
golden, sweet, the violet companion

through the labyrinth of the buildings,
and between them, where the next,
labyrinth begins of corridors and
corners I saw a massive stone, simultaneously natural
and shaped, I thought, 'a monument
to the venture,' and loved it   where the heart
could be carved in reality on the breast of it,
a small pendant stone without a necklace   swings in the breeze

*   *   *

every child knows that China lies in
the West. *The Northwest Coast was a dominion, a future sphere of*
empire, whose distance at once shaped its development and kept it
secret from the wider world until the late eighteenth century.
Fifteen hundred years before this the Chinese had known of
'Fousang.' They called it the country of the extreme east.

Mooning

Hello, goodbye

you wouldn't know (the (sun

or) moon from you own ass

what did the moon say?
clear and bright in the frosted
air—a slight tick and
sticking under my shoes, what

did the moon say   bright features,
or half of it, from here
the kindness and common
touch of gold and green
and blue tip of the hovered
hedgerow   the eye of the sea
answers the eye of the moon,
great questions of the appearance
of things   what did the disc

say except crackling in fire
which the fingers trick and
let go   changed and fumbling,
to melt and wonder where
the edge is   the half of the
world must have the other
half   of whatever terror

our time found and dis-
membered   and then re-
membered the half of it,
distantly violent   the superb
beast of ourselves   composed
what it could not see—
the other half of it

the would-be flower missing
from all thought, sweet
treat of the unresolved
heart of it—what heart
exists except as relation,
joinment   the paradise
has no substance, but that
is the pleasure of paradise,
no substance, the moon said,
shifting the trees, the stubble,
the sand and the footsteps
the moon said, you wouldn't
know the lack of substance

The Iceberg

I want no summer to melt you
I want no tip to disappear where
I find you—and the largeness
out there, wanders, incomplete,
a constant creation to leap into

'Love' wanders, the speechless
mind of it, all that cost of the
flowers and statues—all that
city of delighted streets and
whimpers   O, the locked heaven
whose gate jangles   I wonder
at the steep of it

then wait, astonished that
the sweet heart grows in some
root or depth—and turns
into ceremonies   there are
the losses of the heartland, light,
sleepless forms against themselves
I repeat you, endlessly—

common, sorrowing, old,
and gigantic
                    this waits
and spits the bird image that
began icily in the distance to
save us, unaware that it lifted,
or was said to, the tip of ourselves

Sock-hop

don't put your shoes on the
floor, but dance somewhere,
loose in the floor-shine

what is indigenous—the repetitious self—the land—
that old flesh we dreamed as if it were permanent?

the glass clusters 'to repossess the dynamic'
like certain flowers bunch to believe
a definition—the bright jug-jug of a reversed
meaning

crocodile smiles, I thought
among bright rocks of what
I return to

return to the largeness of
'the great appearances of nature'
of cities that sound so new
in the morning, the cement gardens, resolute

of the supernatural language and
angelic horns or hounds of the
light creatures, a nodding joy of
creations

the slip of the thing, the dew
or mist at the feet of   the throb
remembers, sullen or not, the
long shining

'sweet,' I said, knowing the
sweat mountain, the turn in the
corridors, and unthreaded
tapestries that tell the horror

the gymnasium breathed somewhat
where we danced the Big Apple
and taught the Lambeth Walk,
shoes off   naked, I am not
sorry to come home

Useful Triads

in the silver mind, accused of *gravitas*
and dog collars, the truth is neither
abstract nor free

simplicity's trick of exactly (!) owes
much, and the 'O's' of grandeur
are bought off with red mascara

it's original, of course, to slip and slide
over the beef and vegetables, simmer playfully
on the home-plate

you're astride something, if you pee
powerfully and it tinkles in the depths
splattering the awesome

do you think it possible (when it
has no referent) to point straight
or kiss the crooked or some mouth or

another moment's attention steams
in the kettle where black currants
roll with the surface tension

there could be a change of heart,
somebody said, but it was the clock
who does not speak it

let's begin with the academics, peripatetics,
stoics and epicureans: Plato walks about
the painted porch of the atoms

purpose is dog-tired, I suppose, limp—
the dicks wander from one crack
in the world to another, soluble

dong dong dong dong ǀ dong dong dong dong
dong dong dong dong ǀ dong dong dong dong
what time is it?

the infinite faces of the living mount
the analogue and sweet difference,
'in holding the terrain in place'

let's start with something else
and get old carelessly   it was
his nature to be invisible

and that could be anywhere:
'everything takes place as if we
did not exist everywhere'

angels and companions: let's start
with Bacon, Descartes, Newton, Hobbes
and continue instantly

**à cet ultime instant, c'est la supercherie qui
relate la fatique du siècle**

René Char

the tired century and ultimate image
of what we've been through in
the thousands   the night air fills
with a sorrow that completes
itself   no world there or possible
edge, for it collapses the real
trees

cities summarize us, that is the
reason I've loved them and
their early sounds from the train
station   that is the reason to
depart   they were originally built
for the gods

and I worked at the edge of them
with the sugar beets where reason
made cauldrons, and I saw,
not, as John did, a judgment,
but the sweet flesh boil in what
was otherwise summer and
paradise

thoughtless, I saw them, bees
in the skyscrapers   honey ran
golden and buzzed like airplanes
because you couldn't see the
source

the sight goes wounded everywhere,
not where the arrow falls, swift
and sometimes 'wonderland in
the legends of Gilgamesh and
Hercules is a kind of obstacle
course'

'the struggle for life' is not 'among
races or classes as totalitarian
ideologies' suppose   it is among
shadows   who died there in the
century, careless and proper,
in one view lifted off the ground
by futurity, a kind of hurricane,
named male or female but
androgyne at the beginning,
golden mortality left us immortal
repose, a large, crowded reception
in a private house

The Pause

out and wondrous, there, where
I found them   someone wanders,
pauses   'O, it was you, was it!'

who was it said, 'only the belovèd answers,'
that gardens close and walls limit
because they are paradise and untrue

the wall around heaven is untrue, stings
in all the political ferment where I
found it, topsy-turvy, raggedy-ann of

that deadly plaything, thought, the leading
edge of the process, why will you
try to find yourself finite and sure,

the pleasure-dome, and then excuse
its irrealism by futurity, this
desire-to-live does not stop there

you've got a share of it, only the dis-
missed quality is the momentary
now I see 'you,' now I don't

that is the pleasure of the kingdom, old
vocabulary—replaced by the dictatorship
of a sameness

the big, white ball of thought
with its patent leather evening shoes, tap-
dancers that don't need polish until they're

worn-out   like you, I found
them, a radiance, without cause,
like trees, long-life and short-life,

'nothing remains constant,'   I tried
with my love to stop them, to fuck
them, but they are the transformation

of everything, rising into other
things   and 'things' are a desire
big as you are

do you know that Copernicus attacked
and Darwin attacked and Freud attacked
our self-love

the transcendent value of the future
mystification, the death of so many,
things do appear in their own terms, changing

I found them in a mist and a glade,
and a stone, and a shattered wind-
shield, driven to the wreckage of one sweet thought

Moments

Thematicists think it all makes sense

Plato fucked the middle voice

Wilde said, 'Either those drapes go or I go'

bp: 'death words: "what I meant to say was"'

McCaffery: 'abstract ruin'

our battle with the book is our Buddhist battle

Story

John Bentley Mays said, 'This
is UNESCO pablum'
but I loved the man's brown forehead
and white hair   he had been
sure for almost a century of
culture as transcendent, not
conflict

'the universe is part of ourselves'

we have been everywhere, suddenly,
and twisted the clarities into bottles
and casements

it was the lintel concerned us
we walked through and wondered
above us

the larks of heaven perch and nothing

over the walls, the vision gossips
like rivers, and wishes, marvellous,
perishes

we have been everywhere, suddenly,
glorious texture   the chorus added
eagerness, swiftness

intellect whispers, meanders, softly
landed   remarkable ponds and
cattails

the ferns dream as they return
to green   the efformation, the
dis-creation, the kindness of fragments

the larks of heaven perch and nothing

for bp nichol

Romance

the opposite of meaning is not
meaninglessness, what do these big
words mean in the panic, well,
panic means heart   before we had
formed this, it was Pan, my dear,
and tufts of plants   before we had
planned or kissed it, before
we had dreamed the leaves and
historical consequences, before the
painted ocean and storms, before
the water everywhere, drunken and
sunned, stopped us, before the
rock of our spirit, before doorsteps
and fountains and fragments, before
cats and dogs and cities, the
endless footsteps, before sweetness
and mountains, before paradise
and walled gardens, before
streets and manufacture, cars
and desire, after stars and
constellations are probable, we
found it

No-name

let us take shape now in
whatever animus or anima
we have shaped it

'it' is the favourite immaterial
pronoun—no fixed meaning   the
relation

the definition is relational   the
sweet relation   the horror whose
power is perfect

somewhere, sometime, in your
small voice, founded in palms
and swamp-eddies

the grasses gleam   the gleam
grasses, dew and departure

sunlight, my sweetheart, and
green, heartless nature, large
appearances

did heaven have heart and
aggregation to itself in the great
flower?

O distances   space came, immaterial
and time seemed physical   false
propositions

yet, I hear the crowds weep there,
among them, whispering hugeness,
lips and derangement

O, good morning or terror, goodbye
of such kisses   with you, my salutation

The Soul

someday, the windows   the transparency
screams   open and zippers

the last minute—processions—marriages—
meetings   such rainbows or corners

raindrops—the sound of—which
winds slap or wander

solitude   perfect   agreement
disordered

take it this way or that way
upwards and downwards, sideways
and backwards

reminders of rivers, streets,
sidewalks, the pathways

of whatever form, reforming
a definition backward and outward
of this misnomer—

there it wings, homing, dim
or not, flashes, caught, and
then winters,

a slip of a thing, in and out,
statues and stillness, walks easily

the thigh of the thing, between things, golden
and repetitious

surfaces swim, collecting
the depths and inevitable summers of
there-it-is

Desire

the other turns out to be art and
writing

'I want to forget that I met this
life,' 'I want to remember it
always'   I want to go bye, go bye

joyance, (Coleridge), jouissance
(Kristeva) who would avoid toppling
into poetry   but then
poetry does not wish to fall into
theory, but they love one another
when the pure efficacy of poetry
comes into repute
a reckoning

a lifetime spent   thinking
it over and absolute   the absolute
is nothing but love that will not
be denied   also no more
than a clod and a pebble,
dissolute and lutenist

where was the betrayal of the
immutable?

Anecdote

often, I write on top of the
stove's hotplates—elements?—
and leave the notebook there
overnight

the question is: will it burn?
in the morning, it is cold
paper, coldly scribbled on

the next night I do the same
thing   trap of the child
and man   will you, won't

you turn on by yourself, do
you, don't you   say something
almost entirely

almost immortal, lost among
causes and first spoken
moments become

the last are unwritten in
a mazy motion above
ground

what did I think language
did, as I grew up   well,
it pulled me into

and out-of, upwards-of
and downwards-of, the
side-by-side, serpentine friendship

I've known many but few
did more than repeat themselves
the others disappeared into language,

divided from wholeness, they
are, in their language,
desirous and sightful

awesome, sweet labourers
of something

The Ruler

alligator, hippopotamus, fox, rhinoceros
and frog
dog, bear, cat, mouse and badger
in rowing shells   frog and badger
with the megaphones   they're rowing to
a finish

it begins in the womb—with sound—in the tissue—speech
is later—the music of words

your eyes are wooden   where are the
deep pools   the moment of trees
and their suddenness among
thwarted winds around skyscrapers
and umbrellas

your eyes are like wood, yet she
talked to the images of kings and
queens, like everybody else, having
the power to be one

but that was because of cancer
and her eyes yellowed   she had
more life than I knew in her
rowing shell, gently, sweet river

and the images she spoke to were
not small and included the
little match girl frozen and
fiery outside the windows

she of such searching, who felled
the tree and planed the boards—'chuck   chuck
chuck   of the adze'

the ruler is a child's 25 centimetre
measure of the old foot—how tall are you?—
they are rowing in three dimensions,
never to get there

alligator, hippopotamus, fox, rhinoceros,
and frog
dog, bear, cat, mouse and badger,
in the shell of a boat, enchanted,
with honey wrapped up in the intelligence
between one boat and another

Skylights Smoking a Ramses Cigarette,
a Gift in a Pink Box

smoking the splendour, the odours, smoking
a staring colossus across the shining
water, smoking the centuries, his name
on condoms, afloat in the estuary, *that*
beautiful face in Turin, the strewn pieces
of a 90 foot statue, the silver peace
with Khetasar, enlarged on temple
walls, and the love of Hittite princesses,
100 sons and 50 daughters, among them
the magician, Khamwase, smoking the
stolen stones of Karnac, nightless

shadows of colonnades, a forest of
great shafts, crowns, overwhelm
capitals float down the great nave
a hundred men could stand together
on any one of them   the walls could
contain all of Notre Dame with
room to spare   the colossal gate
for the gods with its 40 foot lintel,
weighed 150 tons, must have

and the wars beyond Dog River, the four
divisions named after the great gods—
Amon, Re, Ptah, and Sutekh of many
cities, 1288 B.C., after the rains, across
Palestine to Lebanon, in the last days
of May

at Abydos, his father, Seti I, offered
an image of truth to Osiris, held it
in his hand, and more youthful, at
Thebes, the same image, held in his
hand   the sound of the water, and
he knew terrible curses that did not
work for more than a year in the
heavens or deep earth

out of the inactivity, inspecting the herds,
hunting in the marshes, swift on a
reed boat   the cat claws too wild
birds and catches the wing of another
in its mouth   this terror is praised
and obedient in the company of
the gods who could be more than 9
and younger in the wish of things, in the
sound of three vases of water, in the turn of the head of
a cat

smoking the heart, giving it to the tongue,
ceremonious mind in the guts, removed
and trembling in the pink box, smoking
the statuary, the pillars rise and drift
in the kitchen air, twist of the
elephantine granite, returning the
sweet face at Turin, smoking the
heart of the god that is in every
body, gathered through the skylights by Isis and stars
in the outstretched heaven

after James Henry Breasted

Advice: find someplace where
you can give the / a profound kiss-off,
the kiss of worlds, the kiss of sometimes

about memory: you're a lizard
of such greenness, of such rocks,
you can skip sometimes the deep crevasse

how do you spell? well, you begin
early to take this and that apart,
and then burn them like western novels
in a wicker trunk—on the bonfire

and the fireflies: they fill the hedges,
become Shakespeare and libraries,
which means you doubt somewhat—

I wouldn't, perhaps you would,
like Marlene Dietrich, roll
across how many *chaises longues*—wouldn't,
couldn't, shouldn't—

but then the big basket of flowers,
remember irises and daffodils,
which, I think, are maidens

To whom it may concern:

there are no bones in your jello, so I'll make no bones about the skeletal structure   the lost form is wary, even perky, all in a gesture   my sleep was perfect, dear lost friend, and our dignity danced there strictly costumed   I wore black, you wore white, together we were all and nothing   I am writing to remind you of causal effects and summaries, in other words, of the last time and parties, events to remember   I have dismembered the black, and you, white perfection, what have you done with your patchwork, crazy, quilted, the perfect ski-jacket down and hills of rocky dance-cards   I am sincere, you are sincere   the plunder of memory and places, empty and filled, gardened or wild, in what pool swimming the surfaces O, you were what I wanted, now disappeared and stained with the flow, such substance, such resin, such super-markets, you have disappeared like watercress in the sandwich, so, I recommend you, definitely, infinitely, somewhere, sometime, exactness of daffodils

signed,
riff & ruff

~~Masturbation~~
~~The Hawk~~
~~God~~
Hi!

'I sent my eye out, one in the
day, one at night, to watch my
essential activity, to brighten
what sustains it now

I came upon my hand, the
goddess, Iusas, and upon
the redolent flower, abydos, these,
after the creation and whatnot

whereinto, the bright, black sun
and the learnéd moon shimmer
seas, rivers, rains, wells and
floods are veins of the great
ocean

there is no surface   I did not
commit you to completion, but
made the string-god out of your
upward-downward
jerky motion in that activity

I return you to the pairs   I watch
lovingly in the morning air and
the evening tide where elements of the *overwhelming*
permanence escape into the flux
not to triviality alone, my love, or even
joyous picnics   there is no perpetually
perishing anything   you named
them *joy and sorrow, good and*
evil, disjunction and conjunction,
flux and permanence, greatness
and triviality, freedom and necessity,

yet they escape into the flux of
rains, rivers, wells and seas
I-Am the compassion of the world, and we two are
continuous interpretations

I return you to your *craving*
and zest—the freshness—
my eye is out, one in the
day, one at night, watching
the inward source of distaste or
of refreshment, the judge
arising out of the very nature
of things, redeemer or mischief,
the companions of literal life and
clay in their inaccessible homes'

First Love

These poems may seem quirky, even hermetic. They are not.
But they do reflect a lifetime of scholarship which gave me,
first, pleasure, and, then, a cosmos, and then, happiness. I hope
that scholarship and the joy of it—the helpless quotation of
it—gave greater generosity, a love of this one and that one,
who turned up as helpless as I am. 'Faults and weaknesses
should be made into virtues and possibilities,' as Gene Wahl,
the composer, memorizing tuning forks, said 40 years ago. You
need not know him, but let the other voice name him continu-
ously. He talked in a co-op bedroom, bunks of the sparest ugli-
ness. There weren't enough chairs at supper, though I had
worked for one in the kitchen, tall cauldrons for soup, as you
dropped the bones in, the boiling water popped on the stove
and lit the eye-lids, harshly. 'Take the garbage out!' It was liq-
uid, a garbage can full, which slopped over the knees and shirt
front. I left and lived on tamales and one hotplate, dishes
washed in the shared bathtub. Tomato sauce up the sides of,
shaving, watching at the mirror. Lemon trees of one lemon in a
lucky year—and the piano divided the window from the bed-
room and clap—and he did not know how to, nor did I, called
years later to say he did, selling pedal-pushers. I was cruel in a
room of white-sheet curtains and a toy kettle-drum chande-
lier, striped peppermint colours and in the kitchen, curdled
spaghetti sauce, egg-beatered, on the ceiling, 'rented with
grand piano.' I can't find him—is he dead? I loved him. I love
him, talking of Rabelais. I'll buy the turquoise pedal-
pushers—let me write prose to explain this interchange of
laughing dancers, at the beginning, to get off the Greyhound
bus, one day, to see Euripides' Trojan Women, and there, sud-
denly, were Jimeniz, ghost stories, Proust, pronounced
'Prowst' by the librarian where I came from, for all of Mme.
Larsen's caution, teaching Greek, but it was French that sum-
mer by the fire before the radio at the fall of France.

I weave, finding the first love.

Home for Boys and Girls

the silvery dark, the cry of it,
writing, the couching lion and the
jokes thereof, playing marbles with
jasper—one was how close do
you get to the wall, or the other,
fall into the pit, steelies will get
you out with losses, keeping the marbles,
glassies were resplendent, butterflies,
monarchs of black and near-gold bronze,
clay balls are the cheapest, used if
you're going to lose—or let's play
conkers, polish with shoe-polish,
harden the chestnuts, string them
and swing, hitting the other, spring
games and fall games, of free
children, the unwanted, sent
from England, 1880-1920, Dr. Barnardo's,
when the child first came, he was taken
to a thawing field and told to bury
the dead cow, he dug all day and
used a crow-bar to push the cow
in, buried her, but the legs stuck
up—stiff and everlasting—he
was given an axe, told to return
to the spot and chop the legs off,
the pieces under the thaw and mud,
in the child's mind, everlasting—
and the true gleam of Wordsworth's
children and Coleridge's answer
in the wind's scream, widening loss
and joyance given I repeat:
steelies, pits, jasper and
resplendent glassies

belief

what America and I believed
about that war, armentière,
a room for two and more, maybe,
at the palace, that's 1943 and
this is '83. I can't imagine begging
for the uniform in the face of Coke
machines and sergeants who 'peel
it'—'milk it,' the man said
before I knew how to milk him and

all he believed in had clabbered,
you can hang it on the clothes-
line, in a small bag to make
cottage cheese, dripping slowly
into the dust and sunshine, some
still believe it and justify it by
the elitism of the common hope of
what they believe in, having been
told by the first denominator that
holds things together,   and the loss
of it is terror above the drainage
of Turkey Lake, swimming above the
orchard branches, and the dark sloe-
gin of their angles,   shadows,
desires, and drowned trees before
the friendships
                    no histories and
repetitions were possible, we would
end things, especially strife, for
the peace of it, and truth was
quietness   in the heart of it, we
lived the lie and loved it,
terminal things and round-houses
for repairs

before the opposition
was friendship, before the yellow
ribbons tied things up, and
civilization was individual, and
culture the conflict, certain of
strife and returning streams,
a refreshment where the wind
screams with the hope of children,
backward and before us, anxious,
silent crowds of belief

My Window

of neighbours and pumpkins and
sweeties, private kisses, sky
and wonderful, superstitions
to begin the day, knocking on
wood, rhythmically, musical
breakfasts, soft, boiled,
toasted with currants, intimate
wandering of questions and belief,
the thin skin wanders the adventure
of clothes-off-clothes-on, and
Mattress Mary, across Rock Creek,
out of bounds, summers

'the sounding air'

nothing repairs, but that is the
comfort, flowing in what system,
the sounding air of the mind,
refreshment, the caves, the
labyrinthine moment always
the universe, haunted me like
god, but I was inside that
complexity, in the left wrist, and
wondered, such beauty, I said,
where the human form drifts
in the rivers, puzzles or dreams
the solar origins   'see the islands,
rare or fortunate, the work of
chance or necessity'   'the irrational
is mimetic'   and the sacred,
after I thought it was beauty, takes
place constantly, ends constantly,
to begin constantly, such violence,
such sacred chance, so 'you' whom
I loved would find the crystal
without difference, would form
and reform   the perfection, the
option   and come back

IMAGE-NATION 19 (the wand

I have told many things and want
to tell more in a small time   to count far off,
since 'nothing distinguishes me
ontologically from a crystal, a plant,
an animal, or the order of the world'
simply
        and 'we drift together toward
the noise and the black depths
of the universe'   celebrate the
sudden hang-up of our visibility,
celebrate the sudden beauty that
is not ourselves   careless   unwrapped
(*ducis*)   the solar origin drifts
in the same boat
                what did
dance in this dancer   was
first the difference among poppies and
white horses of advertisements,
the snow-storm and the grapes
from Africa   and the smile, exactly
and repetitions, but joyous, wintering
in Sais, writing memorable letters out
of the shattered various crystals, rocks, grottoes,
leaves, insects, animals, large and
small   'plenitude and enchainment,
wings, eggshells, clouds and snows'

so, to have forgotten, from the inimitable
solar mix, 'unwilling to become a
higher key'   on Bach's bedside table,
Leibnitz's *De Arte Combinatoria*,
at the last minute—numbers
and numbers, multitudes as
the wind is, fish, I had
forgotten miracles and money
in the mouth of, walked by, in
my lanterned garden where the
nightingale, sometimes jugged to our
joyance, various, pitch and
glass of magic grammar
and presentiments—the fabled
universe, solvent and fortunes,
the assiduous sweetness among
other stones

there we have headed for frying pans,
hospitable, and alone, or the same,
voicless in the common name,
scattered colours, earlier shapeless,
a candy-wrapper with a phone number
on it suffices to call the largeness, and
the smallness—what of that & on the
clothes-line, stiffened handicraft
of meaning, amenable comfort—and
Persian cats, where the rugs
flowered   take 'real' life
and store it in the cupboards,
the shoe-strings and decorations
of natural trees—whisper and
whistle of missing leaves—it's
winter—or summer   or some
other time in the great ritual
of plenitude and enchainment

the infinite who belongs to this race
of many things, the gentle death,
ignorance, and innocence last
summer, the youth of it, the
violence with roses and ivy,
sensible words, laughing rose
petal or someone   the inner
music has worn out—amidst broad
leaves and harbours, linked to
the observer,   submerged
or proximous, exactly like that
which he loves, startling noise,
clarity and shadow, the heights
of ourselves equal to our shadows,
night and day, the miracle of
many things, the 'proliferation
of geneses'

1. Where is the point of view? Anywhere
at the source of light. Application,
relation, measurements are made
possible by aligning landmarks. Attention. *One*
can line up the sun and the top
of the tomb, or the apex of the
pyramid and the tip of its shadow.
This means that the site may
not be fixed at one location.

2. Where is the object? It too must
be transportable. In fact, it is,
either by the shadow that it casts
or the model that it imitates.

3. Where is the source of light?
It varies, as with the gnomen.
It transports the object in the
form of a shadow. It is the
object; this is what we will
call the miracle.   ) Serre
most beautiful   stars, balls,
tinsel, bubbles, red water, the wand

The Art of Combinations

'we conclude with cosmography, the
connection of subjects to each other'
'consumed in the overwhelming
existence'
nothing simpler than what I have said because
I didn't say it, nothing simpler than what
I have said, because I said it—

Ah.

under you, over you, on you,
about you, slaked in a desert, the
pools, the shadow of a face,
a perfect answer, it was not
myself I could not imagine, it
was the substance of no understanding,
leaning over the waterfront, going
out to sea, of honey and milk and
crackers

on the other hand, founded on
actual existence   the pool played
with its ripples widening to the edge,
growing the watercress, the
iced surface, the dinner table
sparkled with lamps, and the
silver moon waned into happy
nightingales and bright forests

honestas

what do you think of that building
without knowing the architect   knowing
the architect, what do you think of
that building   the answer:
they have expanded cheaply,
beautifully, or otherwise in the
streets, holes and parking places

the fire which consists of burning iron,
discovered early, *is like iron*
itself   love is that unity with the happiness
of another   mind and body, such
pools,   winged fishes

'a' is a fig and reducible
'o' is the same thing, shamed
in the garden   what do you
think of that garden without
knowing the gardener   knowing
the gardener, what do you think
of that garden   the answer:
the glass perfectly dark, or
burning in pieces

Epitaphics

Tarzan keeps saying, 'ombawa,'
and everybody does everything
including the elephants

'Wow!' she said, 'I'm out of the
rabbit hole and it's the same.'

'If there's one thing Harry learned
to love more than the sacred, it was
the sacred in ruins.'

IMAGE-NATION 20 (the Eve

wisdom shattered, gold, myrrh, and
incense scattered over the floor, toys
of one thousand nine hundred and
eighty-three years, impossible
to worship the child of what
we are, then what was He in
that imagination? whose perfection
withered the tree to begin with, He
was, first, not a goodness, *that*
we would compose, perhaps, in a life-time
again and again, He was, first,
a cosmos, entered somehow
(by ear?), this hang-up in the
flow, and was named He by
accident in the curious, disappearing
anthropomorphism, could have been
anything in the young, marvelous,
dangerous beginning, somewhat
familiar, neither inside nor
outside, it was that peculiar
cause of imagery, following
a star, that required intimacy,
caught the mind and the cities,
one by one, then in multitudes,
sounds like a great wind or the
lights of the raindrops
on darkened skylights, somewhere
the love goes by happiness and sorrow,
neither one nor the other alone or
separate, neither one nor the other
the truth of what they called Him,
who is incomplete, created dark and
light of
          gold, myrrh and incense
listening to the radio from Golan
and Baden and Cypress

Silver-winged red devil, a toy from Mexico

the place is poisoned   history is effective,
not progressive   date: anytime, or
the Cheyenne massacre and freezing, 1879,
date the re-entry and then the return
from the womb of mankind   it is
not the womb of woman, nor is it
the Greek male-womb, the substitute
of it—books, letters, language
it is our violence—that inside of
ourselves, which gods inhabit,
though they are real outside the inside,
continuous grass, repeated sand in the
glass of sky-scrapers, golden, sunning,
melted forms, banks on rivers of
our violence   I have thought the intellect
sweet and the bare-forms of poets,
hairy-wrists, graceful, the stench and
the beauty, bright and terrible, crabs
in the hair of their chests or the clean
smooth flesh variable   I
sometimes thought they were priests or
the same thing, revolutionaries, I thought they
were baseball players, lovers
or beauties   they were at a loss
in the language, ever so much
at cross-purposes in the world
of that violence which is our nature,
endlessly before us, where
the inside turns into the outside, dying
and other   now, knowing the
source does not look like ourselves,
virgin and child in the icon
sit in a tub of blue weather,
two rivers pour into *okeanos*
where fish begin the dangerous
beginning, somewhat
familiar, the peculiar cause
of imagery somewhere   if you
pound the table the wings shiver,
silver, on springs at the shoulders of
the red body

Image-nation 21 (territory

wandering to the other, wandering
the spiritual realities, skilled in all
ways of contending, he did not search
out death or courage, did not
found something, a country,
or end it, but made it endless,
that is his claim to fame, to
seek out what is beyond any single
man or woman, or the multiples
of them   the magic country that
is homeland

the bridges   I strained for, strings
of my vastness in language, and
the cars rushed by in both
directions flashing at one another

the mechanic of splendour, sought
after, chanted in the windy
cables   and the river sailed,
haphazard, under the solitude

he had only the stories to tell, naked
and plotless, the spiritual territories,
earth-images and sky-maps, dark
at the edges

the mechanic of the marvelous dreamed
of Stalin and Hitler and the ordinary,
endlessly knew where he had gone
and, then, came back, whatever happens
if, I said—I was talking to religionists—
you gain social justice,
solve the whole terror, then where
is god?   certainly not in happiness
and since god is not in unhappiness,
there you have it   the skilled
adventure in hostilities with no name

Dream

I went madly to sleep, dreamed
of everyone, Reagan offered me a dish
and Trudeau and I compared tuxedos,
Rabelais arrived, absolutely nasty,
I liked him best and waited quietly
for Montaigne, the sweet friend

Pain-fountain

the light striking the near and the
far   the sorrow is cultural   the personal
is time in its space, mental and jobbed
large in mischief, large in the gathering
field, gathering the argument and all
its pieces, outside the work, the
exergue, the space on the page,
the outside   what profit from the irreducible
loss

if space is identical with mind,
then, what's in the mind?   a
dangerous freedom—the space may
be tawdry   mixed with the beautiful,
that's the par of exchange,
twisted gold and only similar

                        maggots
and honey, bones and rags, clean
as a whistle   and drifted steel
wonder and go
                    O, he said, as the
fountain lifted each particle of light
and let the gathering heart splash
on a glittery pavement

Dream

       'standing everest,'
flowers they were called—
toilets and monumental
garden planters filled with
them   they were tall, stemmed,
purple straw-flowers—and
the pun, Everest is a mountain,
the sound blurred to ever-rest
standing-ever-rest—

Utopia

whatever it's a sign of—that
trip of   an art
of—
        we're interested finally
in the unique of its meta-
physic
            every anti-metaphysics
reverts into a metaphysics,
as Marx and men and women fucked their
physics

each move is infinite, troubled
by how it got there, the split-
rope of

Freud found it and made sexual
metaphysics, until, years later,
it reverted and made meta-
physics—it's funny that way,
where it walked on the land,
America, France and Russia,

and became not-a-place
but a change of typewriters,
which alphabet or hunting dog

knew better and reverted into sheer
picture or postcard of the moon
over any Miami you can think of

the 'mindless revelers' dream—
America is Europe's dream, its
superstitious futurity

America did not exist; and it exists
only if it is utopia, history on the
move toward a golden age   ) Paz

its conflict with Marxism, Europe's
last dream of the future, gives up
the nightmare—its reason—to be delirious

assholiness, my dears, in the wintry
splendour   what was once called
being is complexity—of reunions—
of act—of quality—
                              of the world
I have argued because, in the
complexity, 'we' could not argue it
together

'It springs on you'

my mind plays in the distance,
free, but is not mine, wandering
the syllable, a mustard of bright
flowers, yellowing the airplane's
landing   the sweetness crashed into
the mind incessantly out there

*   *   *

the summer wind came by
so quickly the other day, out
of season, I walked all day
backwards with the snow
on my ass   quickly

*   *   *

                the day and the night
I found them exactly, positively
separate and mixed them
in a bowl   that white mush
became darkly the horizon on
tip-toes over the edge

*   *   *

I'm so in love with art that
it will get me into the next
world, which, as you know,
is 'white mush'

*   *   *

the poet has no part in being,
is not the priest of ontology
from whom Nerval departed
at the gates, giving up privilege
at the lamp-post—

O, sweet, will you tell me,
packing tinned peas and triscuits,
the colour of being

*   *   *

the huge log-boat to be tipped over,
the ships from China, Japan,
Russia, still in the tint of the world,
eddies, silver, gold and pale iris,
lights tip their cargo cranes,
the moon up before darkness
with an edge missing, all near
geraniums

*   *   *

I have tried for 35 years to
redefine sweetness—it is what
they called being—it is not
behind you or before you
or within you—'the goodness
and sweetness of Dante' is
his composition—the language
composes the good, the sweetness
and, by accident, brightness

the truth is laughter

the leaf   twice the size of my hand
23 points
from the maple

O.

the poets have always preceded,
as Mallarmé preceded Cézanne,
neck and neck   that was no
privilege, sweet and forgotten

seated in chairs, the afternoon
marches along with the shadows
which are not bougainvillaea but
northern   I have always loved

shadows as long as they were northern
and moved gently west   like the
crack-up of books, their spines
tingling with notes and stuffing

most people remember the gardens
with cement flowers and the
house going straight up like
solidified swimming-pools or lilies

when you get to the top which
they once called widow's walk,
you waited in nothing but your garden
hat, beautifully otherwise naked

for the wind-swept sea and the dying
sweetness or womb, *declaring the completion
of philosophy*   or the completion of
the human-being in some / a history

awash among silver trees, aspens,
pounded, whispering 'my foos won't
moos' or some other difficult
disappearance of words which were

preliminary notions, laundry of that lovely
absurd summer we wanted so
desperately   the moss was 6 inches
deep   and if you put a cigarette
out in it, the fire would be
6 inches deep in minutes,
when the fire spreads, the trees
totter and their statues wait
in your thought, exactly numerous

Halloween

let pass   let pass
the butterfly

the dark spaces between
larkspur

in the city-twilight
the winking pumpkin

laughter, not a ghoul
or skeleton among them

tutus, and gypsies
in the child eye's languor

sweet, burned face
of imagination

clowns and raggedy ann,
red headed

sweet, burned hands
gathering bags of

smarties and gum
drops

violet, red, orange, green,
pink, brown, yellow and

chocolate   surprise leopard

and wonderful sorrow

Giant

someone stopped suddenly   someone dreamed
slowly   bus-tickets and the ages
of golden heads   deft   in the middle
of nowhere   the railroads   beautiful steam,
high, dripping tower
                              'If you're going
to think, think about somethin',' said Brick-Top,
bless her and Miss Otis's regrets, reared,
like some of us, by bees, atop that mountainous
protean shape,   the sacred vacant lot
of toy cars, a child's labyrinth and twigs
of toy trees, shining garages
                                        silver to the pelvis,
bronze, iron legs on the clay bridges,
each continuous violence flowers in the rivers
you're somewhere less than perfect,
but reading the story

poetry   is   ordinary   busyness

of   bright   things   I   remember

a   barn   dance   2   to   3   years

old   looking   up   at   the   tulle

and   pendant   blue   sparkle

of   her   beauty   controlled   by

the   banging   of   a   broom   handle

hands in your pockets
legs in your pants
take a chew o' tobacca
and everybody dance

such   early   beauty

There-abouts

O sweet spring   of blossoms,
false plums, true as daffodils
or tulips, the dark primrose,
each garden
                you have read
today, 'Aithon'   'blaze,'
the name in the story you
read which way, altered

gods disappeared because they are real
the extraordinary is isolation,
mind is native to it—sure as
the interface—the weather

I drop in, guided by water and sky,
hello   hello   hello—which means 'there'
before 1880   and still does

for Luis Posse

'O on the left'—Posse

'Delphi is a place that the gods left'—Posse

Carmelo Point, 13 June, 1984

the edges shine   gather   disperse
the many minds whisper   their lure
adamant   to converse with the new
bird

            note-note-trill-note-note-trill
over and over
                between minutes and answers

and best of luck, the hummingbird
right at my ear, humming—
and the robin of such listening—seven
hummingbirds—or quickness, the same
twosome, humming at the chive blossoms—note-

note-trill-note-note-trill
grue, waves and this shore
                    from the islands—
Keats—Worlcome—Observatory Point—unnamed
Island—Gambier Harbour—

the children have played paper
faces   the minds go with the sun,
slowly

cool the dish-water and water
the sweet peas and dark leaved,
scarlet geraniums—watch the wild
strawberries stretch in the dry
moss

what do the bees find in the dry
moss—some sweet dryness? or
the black ant on my leg—some salt
wetness

for Catherine Taylor

For Barry Clinton, d. 17 June, 1984, of aids

a circle of bricks beneath Lucretius' tall
Aphrodite who holds her shell among plum
branches—and iris, columbine—your favourite—
columbine, potentilla to surprise you, columbine,
primula Florindae, again to surprise you—pale
blues and bright yellows—white poppies are not
available here—hail! dear blue-eyed
painter

pin-wheel—shimmering wind   pale
yellow movement   and dark red—
dark centre of the wind—infinite
conversation—black-striped hornets
test the aluminum   centre   quickly
white moth, my summer   pink movement
blue shift—orange—white moments—
golden click—streaked purple and blue—
sweet dark of the wind—my hermetic
summer   yes, Sir, Madame, surprise
click—swirl—buzz at the door, my
summer, the territory maps

The Truth Is Laughter

locked out, and at the same time locked
in the look-out   what perfect rose could
I say or write   the Nietzschean brilliance,
who knew that *the best writers understand*
form as what others consider content

Pretty Please

the sharp yellow marigolds on my writing
table, next to the cowboy on his palomino
and the tiger's bright face across there,
broken into a puzzle, but glued together—
for permanence—among green pieces,
just below the cookbooks and the orange
zest of last evening   and on the table
the *radical absence* of the poet I'm reading
or somewhat at a distance as I've always
loved the other   O there were mistakes
when I wanted to be there

and Tereus,

                  I welcome you, tongueless,
and weave the force of that earning, god-like
or somewhat   how win such distance and
forget you   and weave such intelligence—
backwards it seems—

Praise to Them,
December 30, 1984

the robins, returned to
the holly-tree   snow-
covered unusually, search
for red berries   joined by
flames—and larger—a
Common Flicker, 'red-
shafted,' speckled fawn-
breast, long beak of
Picus—the first in
fourteen years—eating
berries in this city-
garden

O fragmented ago—
      early as morning and
boats do draw the sun—
      every time
the human does enter,
      so beautiful—
no reduction of that flux—
      but it does
act, actualist, and so
      becomes actual
spirit   undone
      busyness
of—

I would be there
                    watching
or almost,

but was not

I do not see—
or was not—
                    what
sees me
            drops and buds
of the whole
                    beautiful,
dawn thing—
                        green
stairway
            and
jellyfish—
                blue
iridescent amethyst,
obscene distance

of personal relation

become fire

I thought when I dreamed
I dreamed,
            kept all sweet
depths in the lily
                  of water
opening slowly,
                  a pink,
a purple
        opening
                  each light
flowering   idea
                  or
drunkenness
            I join
you,
      such otherness
of silk flowing
                  otherness
the day grows old
and vibrant
            I live
there—

writing table

'Have you got a toy-box?' she asked on the first
visit—puzzles, the tiger among the leaves—in pieces,
the cowboy on his palomino—odd the dark tail—the
dragon, a water-gun—specific, the cookie-tin for pens
and pencils—eros on it amidst the crescent and green
sunset   O

dancing with radios

when the little blue-bird begins to sing
that never said a thing, 'spring, spring,
spring'

I danced with Ella   kindly Apollo,
hard and hungry—baloney and beans
on the bus   giving up,
coming down
                    you're out there, so do
something—object of my affection   misty
angel, summer sunday afternoon

what different people can do with chicken,
got the St. Louis blues—man's heart
hum, hum, hum—far from me, but love that
man

love your body til the day the evening sun
go down—or left town—St. Louis woman
with what diamond ring and apron—no
way, he's gone away   all of the time,
come on, come on, come on—blue
blooooooooooo   sweet—thanks

frog in my throat—a song—beautiful—
thank you, violins—summer time, livin'
fish—cotton eyes—rich and good lookin'—
hued wings—in the skies—   until
nothin's standin' by—don' cry—

thanks so much—

love musicians—here goes—savannas
I don't understand—heart as big as
a stone—even iceman leave her
alone—like to suffer—hard-hearted
Hannah—pouring water on a drowning
man—put on your pajamas—travel
in your bee-vee-dees—colder than an
ice-cream cone—leave me alone—

but summer touches, passes into rain,
shining, bending the petunias—careless
of applause—O summer whistles—Jimmy
Kiever and Bobely—careless of spelling
as I hear—thank you, beautiful, for
Norman—Timothies and Williams

swell! big and handsome—ne-ne-never know—
your view is crushing, sweety-pie—night
and day—could you coo?—care?—
share?—pardon my mush, would—but
it's you—baby—on you and you,
and you—everybody—
yeah—yeah—yeah——youuuuuuu

thanks——yi yi yi—young, tan,
tall and handsome—that's all you got—
body body body body—ditty—scat—
hum hum hum meditation

rainbows all over your blues—dark-side
of the moon—your turn—let's bounce
on my trampoline

tap dance, Major Bows—with soft 'r's'—O
four-piece summer—
2,000,000 soft-shoe dances and wash-
board talents—   da de da

for Allen Ginsberg's 60th birthday

hard, gemlike flame

I've always liked the idea of the mind as a
frying pan

What's in it is neither true nor false

conversation

Bare-ass, Pretty-ass and Glitter—or
so I describe my neighbors to visitors
I talk endlessly, quickly   they shift
and drift to the window now and again
impatient   a truck drives up, and they
ask, 'Is that Pretty-ass or?'   'No,'
I answer, 'you have to live here for such
qualities to become permanent'

heavy reading

meaning and content exist only in and through the life of the body, to which nonetheless they cannot be reduced, and ... their manifestations differ in level, in quality, in intensity and in time, so that we are referred irresistibly to an organisation, to forces or tendencies, and to identifiable regularities. An organisation of what, forces acting where, regularities connected with what? Something—namely, the soul—is presupposed by or implied in this, and the frankest way of speaking of it is to speak of it as a thing.... In fact, naive philosophical pre-emptions aside, we do not know what a thing is; we only know what the idea of a thing is in a realist philosophy—an idea whose real referent has never been found.

Cornelius Castoriadis'

crossroads in the labyrinth

my soul!

hymns and fragments

texts are processes

        rather then products,

            mind you,

hither and yon

       Den umschwebet Geschrei der Schwalben,
den umgiebt die rührendste Bläue

          heart stirring

'the modern imagination invents itself (and thereby reinvents
antiquity) out of the evidence of wreckage, ... for to scrutinize
a fragment is to move from the presence of a part to the absence
of the whole, to seize upon the sign as a witness of something
that is forever elsewhere....'

        mind you

reading Richard Sieburth

stop

wanted so to enter the brightness,
mother   the *word-robes*
I forget with impatience

I believe I heard language through my mother's
belly   both violent and sweet   and wanted
to get to it

I listen to the train whistle,
the skirt of love flap
against wind   and locomotive
steam

and do not understand my escape
from the dear over-again
whistle and crossing

for Daphne Marlatt

'Mr. Dandelion'

    the dark meant everything—
the breathlessness of
   'please pass'—
I mean
I fought
      'don't touch'—
I'll breathe again
the sweet
      skin,
I thought
      quickly,
and could not—
         'Mr.
Dandelion'
     the voice
said,
   and I
came back

sapphire-blue moon,
                        once

if I think 'I' unifies
                                I lose,
and the feeling overflows the bucket

if I think the aggregate of large numbers of us,
massified, unifies,
                        our hunger
unifies without justice,
                                each alone
and the same

we still dream behind us of a perfected
humanity   a religion of cities   and
take the thought east   the twentieth-
century project, delving centuries of
mind and heart for a new relation among
things,
                overwhelmed
                                to dream again
of *laissez-faire*   going fair   along paths
through the gardened wreckage and consequences
the State and Nationalism agog with redemption   re-
ligions smoke on the hills, sacrificial as
                                        always

a wordy prison does not make a house   word-
less despair in the freedom of words   that
is, if freed into words, to see different
                                                things,
same as any other

                        sapphire-blue moon, once

untranslatable reason

*Si on me presse de dire pourquoy je l'aymois, je sens que
cela ne se peut exprimer, qu'en respondant: Par ce que
c'estoit lui; par ce que c'estoit moy.*

                              an *outward freedom,*
beloved Montaigne,

                  always thinking somewhere else

demi-tasse (an elegy

the silence surrounds me   political silence   where
   the words were deeds once upon a time and space
social silence   where a fragile good composes   bankruptcies
of ideas run through two centuries   my centuries, watching
the poets sit on the shelves,
                       joined by musicians,
painters, sculptors   not one of them weeps
                              the *borborygmi*
of their guts   signals   language in the air,
loud as Zeus among the fractured religions,   answers
now and again, entwining centuries, to the multiple
largeness
             to which, one by one, we return, never at that point,
abject   only different   the curious sorrow of
                              difference
yet here among gathering bankruptcies, we touch
and part, having given or not—robbed sometimes—according
to our lights
             and thinking before we are after them—
after is never a condition of *beyond*, but of comparison, even
of companionship of *of* and *off*—more like a nerve
centre for conductions   inward and outward
        the afterglow of the sky after sunset   some what

      Tiutchev said, *Blessed are those who have visited
this world at its fatal moments*   I think of Serres: that
living beings are born of flows   of Bakhtin's sense
that *the self is an act of grace, a gift of the other*   of persons,
of place, of time   which flow

      I am not whole   not one   but, as Montaigne
said in his essay on friendship, divided

        *I was already so made and accustomed
        to being a second self everywhere that
        only half of me seems to be alive now*

I have only half   am *dimidius* in happiness,
of mixed blood

18 April, 1988

CONTINUING

genetrix, Venus, *voluptas*—'darling,' says one translator,
'delight,' says another—of men, women, and gods—and
a third reads *voluntas*   the will that is free and not-free
in our inclination for one another—restorer, who, under
the gentle motion of the sky's signals, moves ceaseless in the
ship-bearing sea, in the earth's fruits, blossoms and greening,
celebrant, dweller in the life under the sun: the winds don't
trouble, the clouds seem in flight as you approach; for you,
many-coloured earth offers sweet flowers; for you, daedalian,
labyrinthine, dappled, folding, oceanic surfaces laugh, the
sky summons, shining in scattering light   you move, tellurian,
now at the first sight of spring's opening-day, letting loose the
west-wind; you, aborigné of the air's freedom, first
the birds, pierced to the heart by your sway, announce you, and
next wild animals and cattle leap and frolic on the brightening
grasslands and swim swift, rushing mountain rivers, in leafy
homes of birds, crosswise the green plains, you, smiting
every breast with love's lure, bring them to sexual life,
desiring

        you alone govern the nature of physical things; becoming—
joyous or to be loved—depends upon you   at the
border of light, shining—so, I desire
you as companion of poems   language too, physical
among things, desires   *voluptas*   *voluntas*   *genetrix*

GREAT COMPANIONS

PINDAR
SEVENTH OLYMPIC HYMN

for Diagoras of Rhodes, winner in boxing, 464 B.C.

STROPHE

Take in prospering hand   a shining cup
which holds the vine-flow
and proffer it, flecked with foam,
to the young man, who will be bridegroom:
    'Our houses meet!'   True
gold, this pride of fortune,
this feast   to celebrate
a new friendship,   to raise him out of
the guests' envy of
                        the bride's love:

ANTISTROPHE

so, I pour no lesser libation,   this nectar,
this Muses' gift   .   it is my mind's gift pours,
delighting,
propitiation for the victories at Olympia and Pytho.
a man is possessed by the good turning to name him:
another time, the Beauty of the Gift   (of freshness)
looks over another man,   and his initiation.
the phorminx' sweetness and the many-toned oboe

EPODE

accompany us   on shipboard   .   now Diagoras and I
come to land where
                        I sing of
the sea's child   by Aphrodite,   Rhodes, bride of
Helios   .   this poems repays him   who,   out of the boxing-match,
unflinching, fit to be crowned at Alpheos' River with laurel
and at Kastalia,   is mythically larger   and his father
Damagetos, whom Dike gathered,
who both live on the three-citied island,
among Argive spearmen,
near by the headland of far-spreading Asia.

I bear the news   I put the events
straight   for the thought of their beginnings,
from Herakles,
from Tlepolemos first,   wide ruling,
from their father's source, they spring up joyous
from Zeus' disguise   .   they are Amyntorids
from Astydameia's mother-right   .   numberless
errors hang around men's minds   no way to invent

ANTISTROPHE

now or at the finish, not-knowing, a man's best of the gods' gifts.
and so, Alkmene's bastard brother, Lykymnios,
came from his mother's rooms at Tiryns, Midea's,
to die   struck down by the hard wild-olive staff,
embittered, the raised hand of Tlepolemos,   who founded
this island   so mania enters the mind's skill
and drives the knower to wander off   .   he went to ask the god's voice.

EPODE

in the adytum   fragrance,   the Golden-Haired One
spoke   of his ships' sailing   straight out of wave-breaking Lerna
to that sea-girt grassland   where
the king of the gods, once   let fall a gold-storm,
gold snowing   .   the high brightness drenched the city,
the smooth-bronze axe cut   .   Hephaistos' handwork.
Athena,   out of the crown of her father's head, sprang
joyous   shouting   called out.
Awe wakened Ouranos and the mother Gaia.

and the daimonion,   the light-springing,   Hyperion's
son, commanded his loved children to guard
over the event,   mindful of the debt,
first founders of the goddess' altar   in clear view
and the holy offering set in place,
kindling the heat of the father,
stirring the maiden of the whistling spear   .   Prometheus
and Aidos,   who measure with awe,   caught men up
with prowess   and the joy acts inward and outward
          from the first thought.

ANTISTROPHE
unexpected,   a cloud intercepts us   nearby Lethe
the virtu is lost   out of place
in us   into the air
they did not carry the sperm-fire   when they climbed the high hill
no glowing ash at hand   .   without fire, they prepared her grove.
above the Akropolis,   Zeus gathered the clouds,
pale-yellow, and sent a gold rain upon them,   and the Owl-Faced,

EPODE
glaring, silvery,   sent along companion-gifts,
every art,   and they surpassed all the men of the earth
with the skill of their hands   .   shaped as if life caught them
and motion,   their works lined the streets   .   word
spread far and wide   .   art's language
discloses powers without trickery   sophia   when
men tell old legends.   when Zeus and the deathless gods
chose shares of the earth, Rhodes was not yet
seen in the sea's open water,   the sea-land hidden in the salt-deep.

Helios was gone   and no one pointed to his share of it,
no place was apportioned   .   so the sacred Sun
was left out   he questioned   and Zeus settled
to recast the lots   .   but Helios stopped that
when he looked down into the gray-clear sea.
he said   I see the mantle swelling   out of the sea-floor,
I see my lot rising   abundance for men
from gaia and hillsides for good flocks.

ANTISTROPHE

quickly, he called Lachesis of the gold-bound hair
to raise her hands   to swear   by the high oath of the gods,
without double-talk
bending her head along with the son of Kronis: the island
would be his share,   left to him alone   after she shot up
into the bright air   .   the talk over   .   from where
he looked down, his desire fell to meet her   budding against the sea-spray,

EPODE

the sea-land is held by the dazzle of the sun-flow,   father
who reins the hard-breathing horses' fire   .   they mixed,
and Rhodes bore seven sons,   who take up
his gift of thought,   most knowing among the first men,
as their father gave pieces of land from gaia   to Kamiros and the first-born
Ialysos, and to Lindos,   divided three ways,   wide apart
with cities named for them   and three rock-seats.

STROPHE

it let loose   the outcome of bloodshed   (the other face) turns the
hardship to sweetness   :   set for Tlepolemos, the first from Tiryns
god like,
burnt offering of sheep there,   the procession   and Diagoras
twice in the games' judgment stood crowned with flowers,
and four times at famous Ismos   the good fortune   again
and again at Nemea   and rock-strewn Athens;

ANTISTROPHE

marked by the bronze shield at Argos, by his skill at Arcadia
and Thebes,   by the crowds at the old games of the
Boeotians,
at Pelana,   and at Aigina, six times the winner   .   at Megara
the stone tablet tells no other tale   O Zeus   father,
guardian of wide-backed Mt. Atabyrios,   take
this hymn   (the marriage-cry)   set for the winner at Olympia,

EPODE

this fighter   who, among the powers,   met skill's beauty,
matched his own clenched fists   let his gift be in the eyes
of townsmen and strangers   over him,   the Graces
turning against hybris   he travels   straight on the way
his fathers left   aware of the good turn of events
surely   do not hide this share of the gift
of the seed of Kallianax   :   the Eratidai
    are touched by
gods' love,   the city   holds the beauty   of the flower-bringer
Thalia   .   but in a moment,   the winds hit   and turn

                                    bound for

Inscribed in gold letters in the temple at Lindos

ROBERT DUNCAN

the absence was there before the meeting   the radical of
presence   and absence does not return with death's chance-
encounter, as in the old duality, life or death, wherein
the transcendence of the one translates the other into an everness
we do not meet in heaven, that outward of hell and death's
beauty   it is *a bright and terrible disk*

                                  where Jack is, where
Charles is, where James is, where Berg is   is here in the continuous
carmen   O, some things—*di*—breathe into—*aspirate*—and lead away—
deducite!   for the soul is a thing among many

                        Berkeley shimmers and shakes
in my mind   most lost   the absence preceded the place
and the friendships   Lady Rosario among us of Spanish and Greek rushes
from the hedges around the gas station,
                swirled with Lawrence's medlars and
sorb-apples

                                    What
is it reminds us of white gods
                    flesh-fragrant
as if with sweat   the *delicious rottenness* that teems with
the life of the mind's heart   κρατήρ of an agreement, a mixing vessel,
a chasm, a threshold— Βάθρον —a stair of
brazen steps, hollow wild pear tree— κοίλεσ τ'αχέρδου
—between   among
sat down

                        I am only leonine in the
breath of night   awakening blurred neighbors   as your
faces move   Jack writing the Italian underground   *we*
are too tired to live like lions   on john walls   and gay-bars
didn't laugh at the Red Lizard or the Black Cat   as your
faces move beyond me   suddenly Zukofsky joins the language,
now become larger, sharper, more a gathering than the lingo
wherein Berkeley began   the movement

                              the first of your poems
I read: *Among my friends love is a great sorrow* (brought to me
in typescript by Jack, 1946, that we three should meet)—no voice
like it   turns, turns   in the body of thought   *Among*
my friends love is a wage / that one might have for an honest living
   turns, turns
               in thought's body   becomes

O Lovers, I am only one of you!
We, convivial in what is ours!
                                      this ringing
with Dante's voice before the comedy

sorrow   and guide-dance   the courage of the work   the language
is a lion   sentinels are owls   of work's body   glamouring passages
the poem *WHOSE* alongside James Hillman's *thought of the heart*
Jess tells me you just went, having the heart to   whose
heart?   I wish to say mine   impertinence   yours   that too
is impertinence   nevertheless, always against the heart
failures: *cowardice, nostalgia, sentimentalism, aesthethicizing, doubt,*
vanity, withdrawal, trepidation
                                      fierce, you
      name many times this uprising
—*political, mental, sexual, social*—*you name it*—*mounting rung by rung*

      this climax   to what overview   ·

            under the double axe
                                      whose heart

the lilies burn   rose-orange and yellow   buds about to,
with a touch of blood   near imagination of Blake's Eternity,
except one would be among them   flaming into one another,
not looking out there at the table, the vase, the tall, leafy stems
blossoming
                  stopped over the 'Instant Mythology,' knowing
an old language from you   one-inch capsules in the hot water
break at both ends, then burst   purple, green, red, blue,
'pour enfants ages 5 ans et plus, pas comestible, chaque
capsule peut contenir: Centaure, Dragon, Pégase, Licorne,
Sirène—calling—mettez la capsule dans l'eau tiède / chaude
et regardez un caractère mythologique apparaître'   techno-myth
translates out of the real book into the way language
works   regardez!
                  the travois of the poetic mind,
the drag-load harnessed to the body,   fireily, through

the glowing flowers   warm and hot, the watery spell of
any reel of language   *poluphloisboíous sea-coast*

    window-rain is *Heimat*   sunlight travels the fingers
come subito lampo   a sudden lamp in the room outside
strikes the fir tree   horizon of eyes through passages,
sublime envelopes, and the *lives raging within life*

There is no exstacy of Beauty in which I will not remember Man's misery,
compounded by what we have done   sighted in ruins, neither old nor dis-
continuous
                  (I smile   it is the thought of you   a happiness
that could not be without your having been
                                    there
quarreling)

        the permanent wall of our shape   the languages
burn and muse   the alpha-beta, like the yellow birds
(Dendoica petechia—Parulidae) disappear among spring yellowing leaves,
pricklings, of the holly as its tree renews toward winter robins
and *staerlinc*   wait for red berries where the inkberry is
eastern   the cherries are white among the greens, this side
of glass towers with bicycles on the balconies almost rented the bicycle
on the 37th floor   and figs like testicles on the branches enjoy
the sexual sun

    I remember the quarrel over experience—on Greene Street—
and still think you spoke too soon of a sacred cut-out   it was the process
of the actual we were both about
    what exactly do we experience in poēsis
over the neat 'I' that thinks itself a unity of things or disunity des-
perately untrue to whatever we are tied to—like one's grief or the smother-
ing domestic realism, or the I-feel, so deep and steeply, no one wants to
listen without a drumhead   positivisms of the self
that die into an urn   yet, *O gratefully / I take the gift of my daily life!*
the accusations were: 'fatuous,' 'rhetorical,' 'pretentious,' 'bourgeois
interior decorator' (of Pound), continuous writing of the ironing board,

the kitchen, recipes, the jam pots *textures, tones, tastes* of the world
they are not glabrous, nor is the skin, *riding the earth / round into the
sunlight again* one wishes the positivities were *falling into that Nature
of Me / that includes the cosmos it believes in* how curious, not sad, of
all animals, not merely

you came here in 1982 to read *Ground Work*
up to that point no one could leave the room of *cat's fur, black
stone,* and *its electric familiar What Is*

*mind-store mind-change mindful mind-life Eternal
Mind the smile*
the burn
not to
want any longer to wait for the thematic release

thinking of you thinking of James Hillman thinking of Corbin—
*the idea of a unified experiencing subject vis-a-vis a world
that is multiple, disunited, chaotic. The first person
singular, that little devil of an I—who, as psychoanalysis
long ago has seen is neither first, nor a person, nor
singular—is the confessional voice, imagining itself
to be the unifier of experience. But experience can only
be unified by the style in which it is enacted, by the images
which formed it, by its repetitive thematics, and by the
relations amid which it unfolds. It does not have to be
owned to be held. The heart in the breast is not your
heart only: it is a microcosmic sun, a cosmos of all
possible experiences that no one can own*

against heart
failures

I gather as I must images of *independent realities* I,
subjected to the gaze of things, as I think of you

as you say *the etymology is false,*

> > bringing the core,

care— κῆρ—κήρ   together the heart and the goddess, who
is κῆρες plural among things   thinking of you thinking of
Hillman thinking again, *Beauty is an epistemological necessity* thinking of
a sudden call   to climb the ladder of   which you
did not mean   because it does not mean, though
it is recited   *'Never' being the name of what is infinite*

> of cross-ways

> > of brazen

> > > steps

Robin Blaser, born in Denver in 1925, became a Canadian citizen in 1972. He was an integral part of the San Francisco 1950's and '60s 'renaissance' and associated with Jack Spicer and Robert Duncan in the development of the serial poem. For many years he taught literature and art at Simon Fraser University and he continues to lives in Vancouver.

Editors for the Press:
Sharon Thesen / Michael Ondaatje
Cover design: Gordon Robertson
Printed in Canada

For a list of other books
write for our catalogue
or call us as (416) 979-2217

THE COACH HOUSE PRESS
401 (rear) Huron Street
Toronto, Canada M5S 2G5